THE COMPUTER WIZARD

Alex Shearer was born in Wick, Scotland, 'about as far north as you can get without ending up in the sea', and grew up in Exeter, Devon. He went to London to seek his fortune, didn't quite find it, but had an interesting time looking for it. He went to college and studied to be an advertising copywriter. but decided that wasn't the life for him, so after a variety of jobs he moved to Bristol, where he worked as a computer programmer. In his spare time he began writing stories and plays, and in 1979 his first TV script was produced. This was the beginning of Alex Shearer's career of the next sixteen years, as a successful and popular writer for TV, radio and the stage. He later decided to try his hand at writing books, 'as scripts aren't everything', and since 1996 he has had half a dozen children's books published, including the hilarious *Callender Hill* series, as well as an adult novel.

Alex Shearer is married with two children, and lives with his family in Bristol.

Some other books by Alex Shearer

SUMMER SISTERS AND
THE DANCE DISASTER

WINTER BROTHERS AND
THE MISSING SNOW

PROFESSOR SNIFF AND
THE LOST SPRING

ALEX SHEARER

The Computer Wizard

Illustrated by Chris Fisher

PUFFIN BOOKS

PUFFIN BOOKS

Published by the Penguin Group
Penguin Books Ltd, 27 Wrights Lane, London W8 5TZ, England
Penguin Putnam Inc., 375 Hudson Street, New York, New York 10014, USA
Penguin Books Australia Ltd, Ringwood, Victoria, Australia
Penguin Books Canada Ltd, 10 Alcorn Avenue, Toronto, Ontario, Canada M4V 3B2
Penguin Books (NZ) Ltd, Private Bag 102902, NSMC, Auckland, New Zealand

Penguin Books Ltd, Registered Offices: Harmondsworth, Middlesex, England

First published 1999
1 3 5 7 9 10 8 6 4 2

The moral right of the author and illustrator has been asserted

Filmset in 12/14 pt Sabon by Rowland Phototypesetting, Bury St. Edmunds, Suffolk

Made and printed in England by Clays Ltd, St Ives plc

British Library Cataloguing in Publication Data
A CIP catalogue record for this book is available from the British Library

ISBN 0-141-30011-6

1

The Wrong Key

He must have pressed the wrong key.

His dad had told him often enough not to do it. 'Don't press the keys,' he had said. If he had told him once, he had told him thousands of times. Millions of times, even. 'When I'm not there, you don't touch that computer, you understand? It's not a toy. What isn't it, Michael?'

'It's not a toy, Dad,' he would dutifully repeat.

'Just because you can play games on it, that doesn't make it a toy. It's an expensive piece of machinery, Michael. What kind of a piece of machinery is it?'

'An expensive one, Dad,' Michael had said.

'Don't say it like a parrot,' his dad had said. 'Say it as if you mean it.'

Michael would have liked to ask him how he knew that parrots didn't mean what they said. Parrots might be very sincere for all Dad knew. But he wisely refrained from doing so.

'You're welcome to use the computer so long as there's someone here to help you, Michael. But you mustn't put it on by yourself.'

'No, Dad,' Michael had agreed, his fingers itching to get at the keyboard for a quick game of *Gumbles Go Next*.

'Computers are easily damaged, you see. And if you start playing around with the keyboard, anything could happen.'

And it had. And now there he was. Stuck inside the computer.

He definitely must have pressed the wrong key. Perhaps it was that one with the funny symbol on it which had caused the trouble. But whichever one was responsible, it was a very bad situation to be in. Very bad indeed.

For one thing Michael hadn't had his tea yet, nor done his spelling for another. And he hadn't even started to practise the tune on his recorder. His mother had collected him and his sister from school, the same as usual, and when they got home, he had gone into the living room to watch the television. But the programme hadn't been very interesting. It was too young for him. All right for Emily, of course, because she was much

2

younger than he was, and so she had a smaller brain. She was only five, after all. But he was bored. He called to his mother who was getting their tea ready in the kitchen.

'Mum!'

'What?'

'I don't want to watch television!'

'Miracles do happen then!'

'Eh? What?' It was plainly some kind of grown-up joke. Adults were always saying that children's jokes were stupid, but you should have heard theirs. Talk about unfunny. Adults were always telling unfunny jokes, and then they'd sit about laughing at them for hours on end, till their eyes watered. Childish, that's what it was.

'So what'll I do then?' he asked.

'Well, don't ask me,' she said. 'Amuse yourself somehow. Use your head.'

'What, you mean like bang it against the wall?'

'Don't be cheeky, Michael,' she told him. And that was another thing. Adults were always telling you not to be cheeky, but you got more cheek from adults than from anyone else. Like his mother, always on at him to put his pyjamas under his pillow and tidy up his room. What a cheek. If he'd told her to tidy up *her* room and to put her pyjamas under *her* pillow she'd probably have had a fit.

'I don't know what to do,' he said.

'Well, I'm not an entertainment centre,' his

mother said. 'Amuse yourself. You've got plenty
of games you never play with.'

'I'm bored with them.'

'Jigsaws you never do.'

'I've done them all.'

'Books you never read.'

'I've already read them.'

'Then read them again.'

'I already have. When it was raining. I read
them so much they got holes in them.'

'Then use your initiative,' she said.

'What's that?' Michael asked her.

'Look it up in the dictionary,' she told him.
'That'll be something to do.'

So, you see, it was all his mum's fault really. If
it hadn't been for her, he wouldn't now be stuck
inside this computer. And he hoped she'd
remember to tell that to his dad when he got
home.

The thing was that there was a dictionary inside
the computer, an electronic one. It not only told
you what a word meant, it told you whether
you'd spelled it correctly and suggested three
other words to use which meant the same thing.

He felt sure that he knew how to use the computer dictionary. He had used it with his father
often enough, and could just about remember
the right instructions for it – more or less. So he

sneaked into his dad's study and turned it on.

The study was really the spare bedroom, but his dad liked to call it his study, even though he never did any studying in there. All he ever did was play computer games, or maybe type out a few letters, or estimate whether the gas bill was right, or work out how long it would be before he could afford a new car. At the moment he said he wouldn't be able to have a new car for another twenty-seven years. Michael thought his dad's wages didn't really seem a great deal better than his own pocket money.

Michael remembered the first part of what to do without any problem. Simply turn the computer on, sit there and wait for something to appear on the screen. Then all you had to do was to type in the right word, and you were away.

Only what was the right word?

He had tried quite a few words before things went wrong. He tried START, but that didn't work. Then he tried GET-ON-WITH-IT. Then STUPID. Then he had a go with SPELLS. He thought that would be a good word to get the dictionary program started, forgetting, of course, that SPELLS is a word with more than one meaning. The computer had begun to work then. A second after he had typed in SPELLS, the computer had displayed a message on the screen saying SPELLS PROGRAM LOADING.

Michael wasn't sure what this meant, but he took it to mean that the computer was finding its dictionary.

The next message to appear said SPELLS PROGRAM LOADED. TYPE IN YOUR SPELL.

Well, it was obvious what that meant. It meant that Michael was to type in the word whose meaning he wanted to know. The computer would find it and then tell him what it meant.

Now, what was the word again that he was supposed to look up? What had his mother said? Use your – what was it now? Use your insight, was that it? No. Use your napkin? No. She was always saying that, but that wasn't it. Use the soap? No. Use your head? No. Use your common sense? No, but it was something like that. Use your brakes? No, that was for when he was riding his bike. Use your fork then? No, that was for when he was eating peas. Use your hanky? No, that was when he – no.

Initiative! That was it. Use your initiative!

Right. Now how to spell it? He didn't have to get it exactly right, just close enough to give the computer an idea, and it would do the rest. They were clever things, computers. There was nothing they couldn't do if they put their chips to it. His dad had told him that computers had chips inside, and explained that a computer's chips had nothing to do with the fish and chip shop either, so no stupid jokes. And then he went and made about seven million stupid jokes himself, all about chips and computers, and about putting salt and vinegar on your computer to make it go faster and stuff like that.

But how to spell it though? He said the word out loud a few times to get the sound of it.

'Initiative. Initiative. In-it-ia-ti-ve.' Right. He was ready. First he had to tell the computer that he wanted to find the word.

So he typed in GET.

Then he needed to tell it which word to get, and he began to type INIT – and that was when it all went wrong.

That was when he must have pressed the wrong key. He didn't know which one it was, all he knew was that at one moment he had been sitting in front of his dad's computer, typing GET INIT, and the next he had pressed the wrong key, and he wasn't there any more. He was inside the computer, looking out.

GET INIT? He had GOT INIT all right.

And he hadn't even had his tea.

2

Where Are You?

'Michael, Emily! Your tea's ready!'

Mum was calling them. He heard the living room door bang as his sister left the television and made her way to the kitchen and to her plate of fish fingers, chips and peas. He could hear her say, 'I'm starving.'

Michael should have felt hungry too. But he didn't somehow. It was funny, but once you were inside the computer, you didn't really feel hungry at all. He tried to tap on the screen from the inside, but it didn't seem to make any noise. Maybe that was because he had got so small. He had shrunk so much he was no bigger than a character in a video game now. He peered out sadly. There, out in front of him, was the desk and the keyboard he had been sitting at. And there, behind them, was the study door, and the calendar on the wall and a bookcase with his dad's books.

His mother shouted again. 'Michael! Tea's ready! Come and wash your hands!'

But there was no way he could wash his hands here, not stuck in a computer. And there was no way he could get dirty either. He tried to shout back.

'Mum!'

But his voice sounded so very small and thin, and he doubted that anyone would have heard it, even if they had been standing right next to him.

'Michael!' There was a trace of annoyance in his mum's voice now. 'Michael, where are you?'

'I'm here, Mum,' he said, 'I'm about two centimetres high, I think, and I'm stuck inside the computer.' But of course she didn't hear him.

'Michael,' she was shouting from downstairs. 'If you don't get here immediately and have your tea, I'm going to get very angry!' She sounded angry, too. In fact, inside a computer was the best place to be when your mum started getting angry. Then he could hear her looking in all the rooms.

'Michael? Are you in here? Michael?'

Her voice sounded worried, not angry any more.

'Michael? Are you all right?'

Then the back door opened and she had gone out into the garden. 'Michael? Are you there?' But he wasn't. Then the door closed again and footsteps came up the stairs. 'Michael, are you in the toilet?' Oh, if only he was. 'Michael, are you in your room?' Oh, if only he could be. Then 'Michael, you're not in your dad's study, are you?'

The study door opened, and there she was. He could see her on the other side of the screen. He could see her looking around the room for him, until finally she realized that the computer was turned on. And then she looked at the screen and saw him.

And then she screamed.

Very loudly.

3

No Tea

'Michael!' his mum yelled, pointing a finger at him. 'Come out of that computer at once! Your dad'll go purple when he gets home and sees you in there. You know what he's said to you often enough.'

'It's not that simple, Mum,' Michael said. But she couldn't hear him. She collapsed into the desk chair in a state of shock and stared at the screen. It was Michael right enough, and yet it wasn't Michael. It was as if someone had squashed him and turned him into a video game character. Somehow he seemed to be made out of tiny squares of colour, little dots, as though it wasn't really Michael but just a picture of him.

'But what are you doing in there, Michael?'

his mum asked. The little figure on the screen shrugged its shoulders and pulled an apologetic face.

'It's not clever, you know,' she said. 'Getting inside people's computers. I don't think Mr Pomeroy would like it.' Mr Pomeroy was Michael's teacher. 'And I don't know what your dad's going to say.'

She stared at Michael for a second.

'Well, you got in, but do you know how to get out?' The little figure shook its head. He didn't even know how he'd got in, did he?

'So you're stuck, are you?' The little Michael on the screen nodded sheepishly.

'Well, I can't see you going to school tomorrow.' No, that was probably true, Michael hadn't thought of that. 'Not unless we take the computer round there and set it up on your desk, so that you can listen to the lessons.'

This idea quite appealed to Michael. It would be good fun, being in class, inside a computer. Especially if it was raining.

'I really don't know what your father's going to say. I just hope you haven't damaged any of his files in there, that's all. Because he's got the monthly household accounts in that computer, you know, Michael. And the membership list of the judo club. And if you go and mess up his gas bill estimates, he's not going to be very happy.'

The little Michael on the computer screen

12

looked glum and he felt glum, too. He felt that his mother wasn't really being all that sympathetic. After all, here he was, the only son she had, stuck inside a computer with no immediate prospect of getting out. All that she seemed bothered about was him missing school tomorrow and what his dad was going to say.

'Well, I'll just have to take the day off work then, I suppose,' his mother said. 'I'll just have to phone and tell them I can't come because you're stuck in the computer. Because I can't leave you in the house on your own, can I? I don't suppose you'll want your dinner now, either. More good food wasted. Oh well, the cat'll have your fish fingers, so at least they won't be thrown away. But I can't see him having the peas. Cats don't seem to like peas. At least ours doesn't. And he certainly won't eat your apple.'

Oh, that was great, the cat was getting his fish fingers now! Next she'd be giving his toys away too. Michael felt indignant. Other boys' mothers would ring for the police. They'd dial 999 and get the police, ambulance and fire brigade round there, with all sirens blaring. Michael could picture the fire-fighters clambering in through the window on a big ladder and levering the front off the computer. While the ambulance crew stood by to rush him to hospital for a check-up and major surgery.

Yes, other boys' mothers knew a real

emergency when they saw one. But his mum just carried on as though boys getting stuck in computers happened all the time and it was no more serious than dandruff.

'Well, I'd better go down and see how Emily is,' she said, 'and put the washing in the tumble drier. I'll be back shortly. Have you got anything to do in there, Michael? Don't go wasting your time will you? Or getting into bad habits. Try and practise your spelling.'

Michael certainly wasn't in the mood for any spelling. It was spelling that had got him in here. And he didn't know what there was to do inside computers. He felt small and lonely on the empty screen, like somebody lost in a snow-drift.

'I'll go and have a look around,' he said, though his mother couldn't hear him. But she watched as he paced up and down the screen. There wasn't much there at all. A bit of a blank in fact. Maybe he should go and have a look in the Memory. His dad was always telling him that computers had Memory. Maybe that was the thing to do. If Michael could find the Memory, the Memory might be able to remember which key he had pressed. And then it might be able to remember which key he had to unpress to get out again. He wondered where the Memory was. Or if he ever had known. Because if he had, well, he'd forgotten.

4

Can I Have Your Pocket Money?

Mum was just about to leave when the door of the spare bedroom – sorry, Dad's study – opened, and Emily came in.

'Mum,' she said, 'what's for pudding?'

'Won't be a minute, dear,' Mum said. 'I'm just having a word with Michael.'

'Michael?' Emily looked around for him. 'Where's Michael?' His mum pointed to the computer screen.

'He's been mucking about with Dad's computer and he's gone and got himself stuck in there – for no good reason that I can think of.'

Emily approached and peered at the screen. Her eyes looked very big from his side of the glass.

15

'He's shrunk,' Emily said. 'He's only little, like the fairies.'

'I am not like the fairies!' Michael shouted. 'I'm nothing like the fairies at all. Fairies are soppy. I'm not soppy! I'm stuck in a flipping computer, you pest!' But she couldn't hear him. His voice was like the faint drone of an insect.

Emily tapped the screen with her finger. It made Michael jump. She laughed and did it again.

'Look,' she said. 'You can get him to hop if you tap on the screen.'

'Don't tease now, Emily,' Mum said. 'That isn't very nice. How would you like it if you were stuck in a computer and someone did that to you?'

Michael stuck his small, square tongue out at her.

'He put his tongue out!' she bawled.

'Michael, behave yourself,' his mum said. 'Or I'll switch you off.'

She didn't mean it, of course, but an awful thought came into Michael's head. His dad had told him that unless you deliberately saved something first, then it would be lost when you turned the computer off, and you'd never see it again. Well, Michael didn't fancy that, not never being seen again. He didn't fancy that at all.

'I want a go!' Emily was saying.

'What?' Mum said.

'I want to go in the computer!'

'Certainly not,' Mum told her. 'Having one of you stuck in there's quite enough. If you think I'm having the whole family stuck inside a computer – especially when we've got Auntie Enid and Uncle Roger coming round next Sunday – then you've got another think coming. No, if you imagine I'm putting up with those two on my own, while the rest of you lark about enjoying yourselves inside a computer, well, I'm not.'

Lark about! Michael thought. Enjoying yourself? Stuck in here? Call this fun? His mum was mad.

'I'm not enjoying myself!' he shouted to the world out beyond the screen. 'I'm not enjoying myself one little bit! I'm pretty fed up as a matter of fact, and I want to get out!'

Emily was wailing by now and his mother was looking exasperated.

'It's not fair,' Emily was yelling. 'Michael gets to do everything! It's not fair that Michael gets to go inside the computer but I don't. It's not fair. I never get to go anywhere.'

'Look, it's not a treat!' Michael bawled – though, of course, she didn't hear him. 'I'm not in here because it's my birthday, you know. It's not a treat, it's a disaster!' But he was wasting his breath.

It was odd that he could hear them, but they

17

couldn't hear him. It must be because he had
shrunk, and his voice had grown small too. Dad
should have bought a new computer with stereo
speakers instead of this old second-hand one.
Then they would have heard him. If only he
could communicate, it would make all the difference. Or would it?

'It's not fair!' Emily was sobbing. 'I want a
go in the computer! Tell Michael to come out,
it's my turn now.'

For some reason, his mother seemed to think
that this was sound advice. She looked at the
tiny figure on the screen and said in her sternest
voice – the one she used when she wasn't having
any nonsense – 'Michael, come out of that computer immediately.' As if saying that could poss-
ibly make any difference. 'You're just not trying,
that's all.'

Trying? What did she mean, not trying? It was
all right for her out there. Easy for her. People
are always quick to criticize when it's someone
else who's in trouble.

'Why isn't he coming out?' Emily asked. 'He's
not doing what you say. He's being naughty.
Why don't you give him a smack?'

'I don't think he's being naughty,' Mum said.
'I don't think Michael can come out. Goodness
knows how he got in there, but I think he's
stuck. Anyway, there's no point in smacking the
computer. It might damage it. I don't think

18

smacking computers ever made them behave any better. In fact I don't think that smacking ever made anything behave any better.'

At this Emily started to make more noise than ever.

'Michael's stuck in the computer!' she wailed and began to cry again. 'Michael's in the computer,' she sobbed. 'We'll never see him again.'

'Of course we'll see him again,' Mum said. 'Don't be silly, Emily. He'll be here on the screen all the time. We'll be able to come in and have a look at him whenever we want. He just won't be able to have his meals with us, or come on holiday – unless we can get him put on to a laptop computer and take him with us. And he won't be able to do things like spend his pocket money, that's all.'

On hearing this Emily brightened up. 'Can I have his pocket money then?' she said.

'No,' Michael shouted. His tiny figure hopped angrily up and down on the screen. That was so typical of his sister. Here he was, stuck inside a computer – a real disaster – and all she could think of was getting her greedy little hands on his pocket money.

'No, I don't think it would be very nice of you to spend his pocket money,' Mum said. 'We'll set it aside for him, in case he ever gets out. Perhaps we can put it in his piggy bank.'

Mum's words sent a chill through him. She

was talking as if he wouldn't get out for ages. That he would be stuck in here for ever. Yes, he was right, it was an emergency. Someone ought to phone for the police.

'Don't you know how to get him out, Mum?' Emily asked. She had come very close to the screen now and was staring at Michael with a great big eyeball which, he realized with some discomfort, was bigger than himself. It was a bit off-putting seeing an eyeball that was bigger than you. Fancy being smaller than your little sister's eyeball. It made him feel quite queasy.

'No,' Mum said to Emily, 'I don't know all that much about computers, I'm afraid. It's your dad who plays with it most of the time.'

Dad wouldn't have liked Mum saying that he 'played' with it. Dad took his computer very seriously. 'A computer is a delicate scientific instrument,' he liked to remind everyone. 'Only to be used for serious study and for a better under-standing of the world.' Then, when no one was looking, he'd have a game of *Gerbils With Attitude*, *Gumbles Go Next*, or *Numbo-Crumps*.

'It's a pity Michael didn't get stuck in the vacuum cleaner,' Mum said. 'I could have got him out of there. Or if he'd got stuck up the tap, or even if he'd fallen down behind the radiator, I could have managed. But I haven't really had time to learn how to use the computer. Perhaps I'll read the manual.'

'No!' Michael shrieked. He knew from experience that you had to make a lot of mistakes with computers before you could work out how to use them properly. What if Mum pressed the wrong key, just as he had done, and she ended up in the computer with him? Or if the whole house ended up inside the computer? What if everything that was inside the computer got out? Imagine if that happened. If all the horrible little monsters in all the hundreds of computer games got out into the world and became life-sized! What would he do? It would be terrible. Chaos.

'What does this button do?' Emily asked, her finger hovering dangerously over the keyboard.

'No, don't!' Mum said. 'Don't touch it! If you press the wrong one, we might wipe him out and never see him again. Let's just wait till your father gets home.'

At that there was the sound of the front door opening downstairs and Dad's familiar voice calling, 'Hello, I'm home, anyone in? Where are you? Anything interesting happen today?'

5

Dad's Home

'Upstairs!' Mum and Emily called. The next thing Michael heard was Dad's weary footsteps trudging up the stairs and along the landing. Then there he was, peering around the door.

'Hello,' he said. 'What are you doing in the sp –' He almost said 'the spare bedroom' but then he remembered that it wasn't the spare bedroom, it was the study, and he managed to correct himself.

'What are you doing in the study?' he said. Then he saw that the computer was on. A frown crossed his face.

'Why is the computer on? Has someone been messing about with my computer?'

'Yes,' said Mum. 'I'm afraid so. Michael. And he's stuck in it.'

'Yes,' Emily echoed happily. 'Michael's stuck in the computer. See.'

Dad stared at the computer screen and gawped at the little figure. He saw a small, squarish version of Michael, picked out in little dots. It was definitely him, and yet how could it be? Michael hoped he wouldn't be angry. He looked out at Dad's great big spectacles.

'Michael?' Dad said. 'Is that you?' The figure nodded its head sadly. 'What are you doing in there?' The little Michael gave a helpless shrug, as if to say, 'Dunno.'

'Are you all right?' Dad asked. Well, what a question. Yes, Michael supposed that he was all right. Apart from being stuck in here. Dad stared at him for a while, as if he didn't know quite what to say. Finally he spoke again.

'Michael,' he said, 'I hope you haven't mucked up any of my files in there. Because if you've messed up my calculations for the gas bill, I shall be very upset.'

Michael could not believe it. He just stood there with his small square mouth hanging open. You couldn't beat his family for selfishness. No one else had a family like his. There they were, with their only son stuck inside a computer and all his dad could think about was his gas bills and all his sister could think about was spending his pocket money.

Mum headed for the door.

'I'll go and put our tea on now,' she said to Dad, 'I'll leave you to it.'

'What about my pudding?' Emily said.

'You can have a yoghurt,' Mum said.

'Can I have Michael's yoghurt too?' Emily asked. 'He won't be able to eat it in there.'

Michael was livid. He jumped up and down in a rage. That was so typical. Not content with trying to get his pocket money, she was even after his yoghurt now.

'No. One yoghurt's quite enough, Emily,' Mum said. She looked at the screen and said to Dad, 'I don't suppose Michael could manage a yoghurt in there, could he?' Dad looked indignant.

'Certainly not,' he said. 'I'm not having yoghurt in my computer. If you start spooning yoghurt into computers, there's no telling what might happen. We could end up in real trouble.'

Real trouble? Real trouble! Michael couldn't believe his small square ears. Never mind *ending up* in real trouble, surely they had real trouble right now.

'He must have pressed the wrong key,' Mum said, looking at little Michael on the screen. 'It's a pity, because he was doing so well at school. He was going to play football on Saturday. He won't be able to now, will he? Still, maybe they'll let him keep the score. He ought to be quite good at adding up now, being inside a computer. We may as well look on the bright side.'

'I told him not to mess around with it,' Dad said. 'But there you are, you see. This is what happens when you don't listen.'

'Will you be able to get him out?' Mum asked.

'I don't know,' Dad said. 'I'll have to read the manual.'

'Well, he hasn't had his bath yet,' Mum said.

'That's all right,' Dad told her, 'I'll give the screen a wipe with a damp cloth. That should do the trick.'

'We'll let you get on then,' Mum said.

'Could I have a cup of tea, please?' Dad asked.

'Oh, OK,' Mum said. She took Emily off downstairs.

'Bye, bye, Michael,' Emily said as she left. He waved back to her. He was a small, forlorn figure. 'See you again – maybe.'

And then she was off – off to do ordinary human things, like eating yoghurt and having a bath and brushing her teeth and listening to a bedtime story. Things that you did and took for granted every day of your life. Now Michael wouldn't be able to do any of those things ever again. He'd just hang about, like a character in a computer game, waiting for someone to play with him until they got fed up.

Yes, that was a point. You got fed up with a computer game once you'd played it a few times.

What if his family got fed up with him? Bored with him, even? If they started to ignore him? Or forgot that he was there? It was all very worrying. He just hoped that his dad would be able to get him out – soon.

Very soon.

6

Done It This Time

Dad sat down at the desk and picked up the computer manual with a sigh.

'Well, Michael,' he said. 'You've done it this time.' The little figure stood and looked abashed. 'I won't say I told you so,' Dad said, 'but I told you so.' The little figure looked even more crestfallen. 'I'm cross about this, Michael, very cross.' Dad looked stern. 'Go and stand in the corner,' he said, pointing to the corner of the screen.

The little figure walked over, stood in the corner of the computer screen and hung its head in misery.

'I could do without this, Michael,' Dad said. 'I've had a long, hard, tiring day at work.

Frankly, the last thing I want to do when I come home, is to have to start getting boys out of computers.'

'Yes, Dad.'

'Can you hear me, Michael?'

The little figure nodded its head.

'Then pay attention when I'm talking to you. I mean, I know plenty of other dads, Michael, and their sons are all perfectly normal. But I have to have one who gets himself stuck in a computer. Well, I'm not going to take you swimming if you're staying in there, that's all I've got to say. Because if I take that computer down to the swimming pool and throw it in the deep end, it'll play havoc with the electrics.'

Michael couldn't have felt more miserable if he'd been paid to be miserable.

'OK, we'll say no more about it.'

That was a relief. Michael only hoped that Dad would keep his promise. He had noticed that quite often, when adults told you that they would say no more about something, what it really meant was that they would go on about it for the rest of your life.

But fortunately Dad meant what he said this time and seemed to have forgiven him.

'You needn't stand in the corner any more, Michael,' he said, a bit more kindly. 'I'm sorry you're stuck in there. I know it can't be very nice.'

Michael crossed to the centre of the screen and sat down on – well, it was odd, but he seemed to sit down on nothing. Yet he didn't fall. He stood on nothing. When he tried, he could walk up the screen as well as across it – just like walking up into the sky. And he still didn't fall. It was strange. It was eerie. It was great. Perhaps there were advantages of being inside a computer, after all.

'Well, Michael,' Dad said, opening one of his manuals. 'Let's see what it says in here. Maybe we'll find something in the index to help us.'

Dad turned to the index.

'I know,' he said. 'I'll look under S first. Let's see if they've got anything on Small Boys.' He ran his thumb down the list of topics, but there was nothing there. Nothing under the heading of Small-Boys-Stuck-In-Computers. Nothing useful like that at all.

'No, nothing, I'm afraid, Michael. But don't worry. Let's have a look under something else.' Dad turned to the letter G, hoping that he might find something there under G for Getting-Your-Son-Out-Of-Your-Computer, but he had no luck there either.

It took him over half an hour to go through all the manuals. As Dad studied them, Michael wandered round the screen. He found that he could walk upside down too. In fact he could even sort of hang by his feet – though he wasn't actually hanging from anything. He was more standing on his head, in a way. Only he didn't have that standing-on-your-head-feeling, when all the blood goes to your brain and you feel that your eyeballs might pop out.

Dad glanced up from the manuals and saw Michael upside down in the middle of the screen.

'Don't do that, Michael,' he said. 'You'll make yourself giddy.' Suddenly Dad's eyes narrowed and his glasses seemed to grow bigger as he moved nearer to the screen.

'Michael,' he said, in a throaty whisper. 'When did you last go to the toilet?'

Well, a long time ago, as a matter of fact, but strangely, Michael didn't feel like going at all. He didn't feel hungry either. But that must be how things were for computer characters, they were never hungry or tired or needed the toilet.

'Well, I hope you can hold on in there,' Dad was saying. 'Because the last thing I want, Michael, is you or anyone else going to the toilet inside my computer. Do you understand?'

'Yes, Dad,' Michael mumbled and nodded his head.

'Because it won't do the disk drives any good, I don't imagine. I don't think that sort of thing is covered by the guarantee, either.'

Dad went back to his manuals. Mum brought

him a cup of tea. Little Michael lay down. He lay down on nothing, yet he didn't fall. It was amazing how comfortable nothing was to lie on. It wasn't too soft, and it wasn't too hard, it was just, well, nothing. Odd, because quite often his parents would say to him, when he had seemed ungrateful, 'Well, it's better than nothing, Michael.' But now that he finally had some nothing, it was surprisingly comfortable. In fact, despite what his parents had told him, he was starting to think that you were better off with nothing after all.

Dad closed the last page of the last manual.

'No, I'm sorry, Michael. There's nothing in here that's any help, I'm afraid. The only thing I found which I thought might be some good was called De-Bugging. You know, getting the bugs out of your computer. But you're not really a bug, are you, in the strict sense of the word?'

This was a bit worrying, Michael thought. What did his dad mean? Were there bugs inside the computer? In there, with him, right at that moment? He hoped not. Because if they were, what sort of bugs were they? Were they like the bedbugs he had seen once under a microscope at the museum? He didn't fancy running into one of those on a dark night.

His dad seemed to know what he was thinking and tried to reassure him.

'These bugs, Michael, they're not like real

bugs, in case you're worrying about them. It's just a word that means mistakes. Mistakes inside your computer. They won't bite you or anything.'

Well, that was a relief.

'But how exactly did you get in there, Michael?' Dad asked. 'Can you remember which key you pressed?'

It all seemed a long time ago. What had he been doing? What key had he pressed? The computer wasn't pinching his memory, was it, and using it for its own?

'Well, try to remember, will you. Maybe you could tell me, in sign language or something?'

Yes, he'd try.

Dad closed the last manual with a thump.

'Yes, well, that's it, I'm afraid, Michael,' he said. 'I don't think there's anything more I can do tonight. We'll just have to phone the shop in the morning and ask the engineer to come round. Maybe he'll be able to get you out.'

A voice called up the stairs. It was Mum shouting for Dad to come and have his dinner.

'I'll go and have my tea then, son,' Dad said. 'I'll pop back in to see you later. Don't go wandering off, will you?' And he left.

Wandering off? How could he wander off? Where was there to wander off? Michael turned away from the screen and peered ahead. All he could see was murky darkness. What was down there? The computer's workings and its memory, he supposed.

Perhaps he should go and investigate.

7

The Goldfish

'Any success?' Mum asked, as she and Dad sat down to tea.

'No, not really,' Dad admitted. 'I'll have to ring the engineer in the morning and get him to come round.'

'Well, it's all most peculiar,' Mum said.

'Yes,' Dad agreed. 'But I don't see what else we can do about it. We'll just have to leave him in there for tonight and see what happens tomorrow.'

'Do you think he'll be warm enough?' Mum asked.

'What do you mean?'

'In the computer,' she said.

'I don't see why not,' Dad said.

'I could always put a blanket over it.'

'I don't think you should do that,' Dad said. 'Don't put a blanket over it. It might catch fire or something.'

'What about his pyjamas?'

'What about them?'

'I mean, I don't suppose Michael will be able to put them on?'

'Not really.'

'I don't like the thought of him being in there all night and sleeping in his clothes,' Mum said.

'No,' Dad agreed. 'But it can't be helped.'

'What about a pillow?'

'What about it?'

'I don't imagine there's any way we can get a pillow in there, to make him comfy.'

'Don't think so,' Dad said. 'Not that I can see.'

'Oh well, perhaps we can bring him down later and put him in front of the television, so he'll at least have something to look at.'

'No, I daren't do that,' Dad said. 'Because first we'd have to switch off the computer and if we did that, we might lose Michael for ever. We wouldn't want that.'

'No,' Mum agreed.

'I mean, we've only had him a few years,' Dad said. 'You'd expect him to last a bit longer. We've spent a lot of money on him too.'

Mum nodded. 'Yes, children's clothes are very

expensive,' she said. 'He's hardly worn those tracksuit bottoms.'

'That's what I mean,' Dad said. 'It would be a bit of a waste to go switching him off and never get him back again, especially when he's hardly worn his tracksuit.'

'I'd miss him too,' Mum said.

'And me,' Dad agreed. 'Though I do wish he wouldn't muck about with my computer.'

'You should have told him not to,' Mum said.

'I did,' Dad told her. 'If I told him once, I told him ten zillion trillion times, not to touch it when I wasn't there.'

'Well, too late now,' Mum said. 'But I don't like the thought of leaving him in there on his own all night with no company and nothing to look at.'

'Then how about the goldfish?' Dad suggested.

'What about it?'

'We could take its bowl up to the study and sit it on the desk by the computer. Then Michael would have something to look at through the night and he wouldn't get lonely.'

'Good idea,' Mum said. 'Let's do that before we go to bed.'

8

Bedtime

Emily was the first to come in to say goodnight. She found Michael lying upside down in the middle of the screen, with his arms folded on his chest.

'What are you doing?' she said. He turned round and looked at her. 'Is it nice in there?' she asked. He shrugged. 'Are you stuck in there for ever then?' she said. He shrugged again. He wished she wouldn't sound so cheerful about it. 'Can I bring Becky round to see you?' Michael shook his head angrily. He didn't want his little sister bringing her friends round to gawp at him, like a monkey in a cage at the zoo. 'Well, I'm going to bring her round anyway,' she said. 'There's nothing you can do to stop me. And what's more, I'll charge her ten pence to look at you and I'll keep all the money for myself.' Michael stuck his tongue out at her. Then he put his thumbs in his ears and waggled his fingers at her.

'Don't do that, or I'll turn you off!' she said, her hand hovering dangerously over the OFF switch. Luckily Mum arrived, followed by Dad carrying the goldfish bowl.

'That's enough, Emily,' Mum said. 'I heard that. Go to bed now. We don't want anyone switching anyone off, thank you. It's not a nice thing to say.'

'I wouldn't really have done it,' Emily said.

'No, well say goodnight to your big brother now, and get to bed.'

''Night, Michael,' Emily said. He wished he was going to bed too, in his own bed and pyjamas, with a proper pillow. Emily went out of the door.

For some reason Michael couldn't work out, Dad was carrying the goldfish bowl. He plonked it down on the desk close to the computer screen.

'Here you are, Michael,' he said. 'Mum and I thought you might like to have some company.'

Company? A goldfish? What sort of company was that? Stuck in a computer looking at a stupid goldfish all night, watching it go round and round in its bowl, with its mouth hanging open – huh!

38

Dad shook a little goldfish food from a small container into the bowl. Great. Now Michael had to watch the stupid goldfish have its dinner.

'We'll leave a light on,' Mum said, 'so you should be all right.'

'That's right,' Dad said. 'If you do need anything, just give us a shout.'

Give them a shout? He did wonder about his parents sometimes. Give them a shout? It was all he could do to give them a wave.

'I don't think he can shout,' Mum said.

'No, well, I didn't mean shout in the strict sense of the word,' Dad explained. 'I more meant – give us a nod.'

Give them a nod? Far lot of use that would be. Giving them nods when they weren't there to see them. They'd be tucked up in their room together, fast asleep. Snoring too, probably. So what use was a nod? Nods never woke anyone up. But there you were. That was typical of adults. They were always dismissing your problems, saying that it was nothing to worry about and that everything would be all right by morning.

'It'll be all right by morning, I should think, Michael,' Mum was saying.

'Absolutely nothing to worry about,' Dad added.

'Well, 'night then, Michael,' Mum said. 'Sleep tight, see you in the morning.' She looked at Dad. 'Can I give him a kiss?' she asked.

'What?' Dad said.

'Give him a kiss?'

Michael looked out at them. He hoped Mum wouldn't give him a kiss. He had become so small that her lips were bigger than he was.

'I wouldn't risk it,' Dad advised. 'Not kissing a computer screen. You might get a shock.'

'I'll just wave then,' she said. And she did. Michael waved back. Then Dad waved. And Michael waved at him.

'See you in the morning then, Michael.'

'Sleep well,' Mum said.

And then they left him alone with the goldfish.

Michael didn't know what to make of his parents. They just seemed a bit, well – casual about everything. Most parents would probably have panicked if one of their children had got stuck inside a computer. But not his mum and dad. They seemed to take it all for granted, as if things like that happened all the time in their house.

9

A Long Night

It was going to be a long night. Mum left a light on, as she had promised. Not the big one, but the desk lamp, which softly illuminated the room. Michael stared out at the goldfish and the goldfish stared back at him. Then it went off on another tour of its bowl.

What a dull life, Michael thought, being a goldfish, doing nothing but go round and round in circles all day. A bit like being a wheel, really. When you came to think of it, wheels and goldfish had a lot in common. They just went round and round and round. No matter how far they travelled, they were always in the same place. Odd.

These were the sorts of thoughts that filled your head when you were stuck in a computer.

Michael yawned. It was a small, square, computer yawn. But he wasn't tired, just bored. He didn't feel tired or hungry or thirsty, and he still didn't need to go to the toilet. It was a strange life, this computer life. You were alive, and yet you weren't alive. A bit like being a robot.

He wandered round the screen looking for something to do, but everything was in darkness. He turned to face the inside of the computer and walked a little way along. He turned back to see how far he had come and there, behind him, was the computer screen. Beyond it, out on the desk, was the goldfish swimming in its bowl. It was like looking at a television. Only it was the other way round. He was on the inside and the goldfish was on the outside. It was difficult to tell which was the real world any more, because one seemed as real and as unreal as the other.

He didn't want to go too far in case he got lost. So he decided to walk out as far as he could while still keeping the light of the study lamp in sight. He walked until it was a small dot, then he stopped and looked around.

In front of him was a post. It was fluorescent and glowed in the dark. On it were three signs. The top one said MEMORY. The left one said UPPER MEMORY. And the right one said LOWER MEMORY. He was trying to think what the signs meant when he felt a tap on his shoulder. He jumped with fright.

42

'Ahh!' he cried. 'Who's that?' He spun round and came face to face with a small, furry, vaguely familiar creature with a long snout.

'Hello,' the creature said. 'Who are you?'

'Never mind who I am,' Michael said indignantly, annoyed because he had been frightened. 'Who are you?'

'Well, you tell me first!'

'Why can't you tell me first?' Michael demanded.

'Because I'm a Gumble,' the creature said. 'And Gumbles never do anything first. Gumbles only do things second. So if you want me to do something, you have to do it first yourself so I can copy you. Gumbles only follow things, see.'

'What things?' Michael asked, looking at the creature curiously. He remembered it now from one of the games in the computer.

'Other Gumbles, mostly, I suppose,' the Gumble said.

'But that's stupid,' Michael said.

'I wouldn't be surprised,' the Gumble agreed. 'Gumbles are stupid sorts of things.' He looked at Michael closely. Finally he said, 'You're not a Gumble, are you?'

'Of course not. I'm a boy.'

'What game are you out of?' the Gumble asked.

'I'm not out of any game,' Michael said. 'I'm from the big world outside.'

43

'*The Big World Outside*?' the Gumble said. 'I've never heard of that game. Is it a new one?'

'The big world outside isn't a game, it's real,' Michael said. 'It's where all the people are. Out there. In the world!'

'It's another computer then, is it?' the Gumble asked. 'The world?'

'No, it's the real world!' Michael said. 'It's real. Not like in here. This is just a computer. This is all – well – just electricity – and atoms.'

'So what are you made of, out there?'

'Well – atoms, I suppose, but we're real atoms. In here you're just – pretend atoms.'

The Gumble looked a bit sad at this.

'You mean, I'm not real?' he said.

'No, I'm afraid not. Sorry,' Michael said.

'Not a real creature at all?'

'No.'

'Just a pretend one?'

'Yes. You see, somebody probably drew you, whereas me, I was born.'

'Nobody drew you?' the Gumble said.

'No. I came out of my mum's tummy – or something like that,' Michael said.

'So where did I come out of? Did I come out of your mum's tummy as well?'

'No. You came out of the computer games shop,' Michael said. 'My dad bought you.'

'But he didn't buy you?' the Gumble said, looking very perplexed.

44

'No. He got me for free.'

'Oh.' The Gumble stood scratching his head. 'I dunno about this,' he said. 'It all sounds a bit complicated to me. You don't know where the other Gumbles are, do you? I've lost them.'

'No, I'm afraid not. I haven't seen them.'

'That's a shame, I've lost my game. I was in a game of *Gumbles Go Next*, you see,' the Gumble said, 'but I fell out and got lost. I've been wandering round this computer for ages and I can't find the other Gumbles anywhere. The only thing I've been able to find is a program for working out your gas bills.'

'I hope you didn't interfere with it,' Michael said. 'That's my dad's.'

'Interfere with it?' the Gumble said. 'I couldn't even understand it. But I do wish I had someone to follow,' he continued. 'A Gumble's lost without someone to follow. I don't suppose I could follow you, could I?'

'I'm not really going anywhere,' Michael said. 'I'm just waiting till the morning, for the man from the shop to arrive and get me out of the computer.'

'He wouldn't get me out too, would he?' the Gumble asked.

'No, well, you belong here, I don't.'

'Nice to travel though,' said the Gumble. 'Oh well, never mind. If I can't follow you, I'll just have to follow my nose.' And with a twitch of his snout he was off, into the darkness, in the direction of LOWER MEMORY.

'What's in LOWER MEMORY?' Michael called after him as he went.

'Erm – can't remember,' the Gumble said.

'What's in UPPER MEMORY then?'

'It – eh – slips my mind. Sorry.'

'Bye then, thanks anyway.'

And the Gumble vanished from sight.

10

The Bug

Michael thought of following the sign for LOWER MEMORY too, but he didn't want to risk getting lost and not being able to find his way back to the screen. He didn't mind being stuck in a computer for one night, but he didn't want to be there for ever.

He slowly walked back to the screen, the goldfish getting bigger and bigger as he approached. When he had gone as far as he could, he lay down on the dark nothing, closed his eyes and tried to sleep.

Sleep didn't come. He just couldn't feel tired, no matter how many imaginary sheep he counted. And far from being nice and quiet, as you'd expect a computer to be, there were things going on all night and all kinds of odd creatures passing by, who'd come out of their computer games to walk around the computer and stretch their legs.

For the most part, Michael ignored them and they ignored him. Or they assumed that he was just another character from a computer game. He wouldn't have said anything to anyone if an odd-looking insect hadn't hopped around the screen and landed on him with a thump.

'Watch it,' Michael said. 'You nearly flattened me.'

'Beg pardon,' the insect said, scratching her left shoulder with one of her eight right feet. 'Didn't see you there. What game are you from?'

'I'm not. I'm from the real world,' Michael said, getting a little tired of having to explain himself all the time. These computer creatures were all the same. Caught up in their own little worlds, they thought that no one else existed.

'*The Real World*, eh? Is that a good game?'

'It's not a game.'

'Oh, educational, is it? Yes, I like a bit of education myself.'

'So who are you?' Michael asked, as the creature now began to scratch her right shoulder with one of her eight left feet.

'I'm a bug.'

'A bug?'

'Yeah, a computer bug.'

48

'Where from?'

'Well, you know that program about how to work out your gas bill?'

'Yes,' said Michael. 'My dad did that.'

'Well, that program's got a bug in it,' the bug said proudly. 'And that bug is me!'

'Oh!'

'Yes. Your dad'll never get his gas bills right, till he gets rid of me. That's what a bug is, you see. She's the bit that makes things go wrong. A sort of pest really. Yes, I suppose that's what I am, a pest.'

And with that, she hopped off to annoy someone else.

'I'm going to tell my dad about you,' Michael shouted after her. But the bug only stuck her tongue out.

'Have to find me first,' she said. Then she scratched the back of her right knee with the front of her nose, and with one great hop, she disappeared.

11

Morning

It was morning at last. Michael could see the sunlight come creeping under the blinds.

Soon Mum came in, wearing her dressing gown.

'Morning, Michael,' she said. 'How are you? Did you have a good night?' She picked up the goldfish bowl and moved it. 'I don't suppose you'll want any breakfast?'

What a flipping daft question, Michael thought. How was she going to get a piece of toast inside the computer? He shook his head. No thanks.

'I'll be back to see you,' she said. Off she went down to the kitchen.

Emily was the next in. She had dressed herself

in a hurry and had put on her cardigan inside-out, but Michael wasn't going to tell her.

'Hello, Michael,' she said. 'I've been thinking. I thought if I asked everyone in my class for twenty pence to see you stuck in the computer, then that would be a lot of money. And we could have half each. All right? I'll put your share in your piggy bank until you get out.' Before he had a chance to answer, she was off.

About five minutes later Dad came in, bleary-eyed, unshaven, his hair sticking up in tufts.

'Oh, hello, Michael. Good, you're still there then.'

Well, where else would he be? In Australia?

'I'm going to take the morning off work while Mum takes Emily to school and I'll try to get this sorted out. I'd better phone the man in the computer shop as soon as they open. I'll go and have my breakfast.'

And he was gone too.

At eight-thirty, Mum took Emily to school. Michael could hear her chanting as she left the house:

'My brother's in the computer
My brother's in the computer
He's got stuck in and he can't get out
My brother's in the computer.'

He hoped that she might fall over the dustbin, but though he listened for a crash, he didn't hear one and felt disappointed.

At nine o'clock Dad got on the phone to the Cheap And Cheerful Computer Shop. It was Mr Clarke who answered.

'Hello,' he said. 'Clarke's Cheap And Cheerful Computer Shop. For the best bargains in town.'

'Hello,' said Dad. 'It's Mr Riggs here. I bought a computer off you last month, if you remember.'

'Ah, yes,' said Mr Clarke, 'I remember you, Mr Riggs. You tripped over on your way out and landed in the display of mobile phones.'

Dad preferred not to remember this. 'Yes, anyway, the thing is, I've got a few problems with the computer now,' he said. 'It's still under guarantee and you did say that you'd come out and help if anything went wrong.'

'And indeed we will, Mr Riggs. I'll send Frank, my engineer over, straight away. Now you just tell me the problem.'

'Well, it's difficult, really.'

'Nothing is too difficult for us.'

'A bit unusual, then.'

'Nor too unusual either. I guarantee you, Mr Riggs, that whatever your problem is, someone else will have had it before and we'll know exactly how to fix it. So what's wrong with your computer?'

'Well –' Dad hesitated. 'My son's stuck in it.'

The phone went quiet.

'We seem to have a bit of a bad line,' Mr

Clarke said. 'Did you say – your thumb's stuck in it?'

'No, not my thumb, my son!'

'You've poured a cup of coffee over it, have you? Is that what you're trying to say?'

'No, no! My son is stuck in my computer. He is stuck in there, on the screen. It's sucked him in and shrunk him and turned him into a little computer person. I don't know how to get him out.'

There was a long pause at the end of the phone, then Mr Clarke spoke.

'Have you been ill lately, Mr Riggs?' he said.

'No! I am not ill.'

'Any mental problems in the family?' Mr Clarke enquired, as politely as he could.

'I am not ill and I am not mad,' Dad shouted down the phone. 'I am completely sane and in possession of all my senses. So just send the engineer round, would you please, and quick. In fact, double quick!'

'As soon as we can,' Mr Clarke said and he put down the phone.

12

Frank

Dad looked at little Michael on the computer screen. 'The engineer's coming,' he said. 'But to be honest, I don't think they entirely believed me. Well, he'll see for himself when he gets here. After all, they sold me the thing.'

Dad went off to make a cup of tea. By the time he had drunk it, the computer engineer was at the door. Dad let him in.

'Morning,' the engineer said. 'I'm Frank.' He was a cheerful man who carried a small briefcase containing his books and tools. 'Which way to the disaster?' he said brightly.

'Upstairs,' Dad said. 'In the spare – that is, in the study. Would you like a cup of tea?'

'No thanks,' Frank said. 'Just had one.' They

went up to the study and Frank looked around.

'Something very unusual about this study, isn't there, don't you think?'

'Like what?' Dad said.

'I don't know. Just reminds me an awful lot of a spare bedroom.'

'Well, it's not,' Dad said. 'It's a study.'

'Unusual having wardrobes in a study,' Frank said.

'It's an unusual study,' Dad told him. 'The computer's over here.'

'So what seems to be the trouble exactly?' Frank said, putting down his case. 'I got a bit of a garbled message from Clarke's Cheap And Cheerful Computers saying something about you spilling a bottle of rum in it.'

'No, not rum! I didn't say rum at all. I said it was my –'

Dad was just about to tell Frank that his son was stuck in the computer when Frank looked at the screen and saw for himself the small figure of Michael in his tracksuit bottoms and sweat-shirt looking out at him. Michael waved hello.

'I hope he can help me,' he thought.

'Here!' Frank said. He was so shocked that he dropped his briefcase on to Dad's foot.

'Ow! What?' Dad said.

'There's a boy in that computer!' Frank barked. He pointed at the screen with his finger.

'I know,' Dad said. 'I know that!'

'Well, you can't put boys in computers,' Frank said. 'You can't let boys inside computers, they'll mess them up.'

'I didn't let him in,' Dad said. 'He got in while I wasn't looking.'

'Inadequate supervision,' Frank said. 'An inadequately supervised computer is a computer what's going to get a boy in it sooner or later. I hope you realize that once boys get inside computers, they can play havoc with your disk drives.'

'So get him out then!' Dad started to shout. 'That's why you're here. That's what I phoned up for. You're the expert. Get him out.'

'I don't think you're covered on your warranty for this,' Frank said, shaking his head, as though someone was trying to trick him and get something for free. 'There's nothing on the warranty about boys getting inside.'

'I never said there was,' Dad said. 'I just want you to get him out.'

'It might cost extra,' Frank warned him.

'I'll pay,' Dad said. 'Whatever it takes. I can't leave my son in a computer for the rest of his life. He'll never be able to ride his bicycle.'

'Yes, well, I'll see what I can do then.'

Michael sat and watched as Frank set to work. First he typed in some instructions on the keyboard. Nothing happened. He tried some more, but they, too, were to no avail. Finally he opened up his screwdriver kit and took the back off the computer.

'Can you see him in there?' Dad asked, as Frank peered into the back. 'Do you think we could get hold of him and pull him out the back way?'

'No, it doesn't work like that,' Frank said. 'Computers aren't that simple. Computers are very complicated. Half the time you need a computer just to figure your computer out. And even if we could get him out the back way, it wouldn't help. Because he's little and square at the moment, isn't he? You don't want him little and square, do you?'

'Of course not,' Dad said, 'I want him back to full size. I don't want him waddling around like an elf.'

'Exactly,' Frank said. 'You want him back to normal. I mean, he's no use if he's only the size of a baked bean, is he? After all, who wants a baked bean for a son?'

'No,' Dad agreed.

'No. Be different if you had a tin of them. Then you could spread them on toast. So getting him out's only half the battle,' Frank said. 'We've got to get him back to full size as well. That's the tricky bit. Very tricky indeed.'

'But how did he get in there?' Dad said.

'That's a good question,' Frank said. 'It would

be a clever man who knew the answer to that one.'

'So what is the answer?'

'I don't know,' Frank said. 'I'm not that clever.'

'Then who is?' Dad demanded. 'I hope someone is. We can't all be dopey, surely. And you sold me the computer, after all. You ought to warn people before you go selling them computers, that their children can end up inside them, no bigger than baked beans.'

'Didn't know it could happen myself,' Frank said. 'It's a new one on me. But there you are, you learn something new every day.'

Michael listened as they argued. He yawned. It was funny, but he was starting to care less and less whether he ever got out of the computer. He even felt as though his brain was becoming square too. Maybe life wouldn't be so bad as a computer character. It was just a matter of adapting to it. If you stayed anywhere long enough, you grew to like it in the end.

'I know!' Frank said. 'I've had a brainwave!'

'Have you got the answer?' Dad said excitedly.

'I think I may well have it,' Frank said. 'I think I do.'

'Well?' Dad said. 'What is it? Come on, tell me!'

'It's not the perfect solution,' Frank said. 'Not by any means, but it's a way round the problem and it's better than nothing.'

'Go on. Tell me. What do we do?'

Frank looked very solemn. Then, as if he thought he might get a gold star for his answer, he said, 'Easy. We print him out, on the printer.'

'We do what?' Dad said.

'Print him out. I don't know why I didn't think of it before,' Frank said. 'All we have to do is press the PRINT SCREEN button and we can print him out on your printer.'

Michael didn't much like the sound of this. Neither did Dad.

'But hang on,' he said. 'You can't do that. I mean, if you print him out –'

'Yes?' Frank said.

'Well, he'll be flat.'

'Yeah, maybe,' Frank said, in a hurt tone. 'Maybe he will be flat, but at least he'll be out.'

'But that's no good,' Dad said, starting to get hysterical. 'What good's that, having your son printed out? What use is that? What am I supposed to do with him when he's flat?'

Frank thought for a moment. 'Well,' he said, 'you can pin him up on the wall. Or you could run off a few copies of him and have them all around the house. Send one round to his school. Then it'll be like he's back to normal. And you'll still have him in the computer too, if you ever need to run off a few more extra copies. You could even send him out as Christmas cards.'

'No, I'm sorry,' Dad said. 'I don't wish to sound ungrateful, but frankly, Frank, it's not good enough. I want my son out of that computer. Your shop sold it to me and you told me that it was safe.'

'When supervised –' Frank began.

'Supervised or not, that isn't the point. The point is that you sold me a dangerous computer. You should have warned me that my Michael could end up inside it, and you didn't. That's your fault. So what are you going to do about it?'

'How about if we give you a refund of ten pounds? And a free packet of disks?'

Michael looked indignant. I'm worth more than that, he thought.

'That's not good enough,' Dad said. 'I want satisfaction and my son back, or I'm going to get the television news round here and you'll lose a lot of business once word about this gets out, I can tell you.'

Frank looked worried.

'There's no need for that sort of attitude,' he said. 'No call for bad publicity. I'm sure we can keep this quiet and come to a friendly solution.'

'Well, then?' Dad said. 'What do we do?'

'OK, well, there is someone who can help you.'

'Who?' Dad said.

'Only it could be expensive –'

'That's all right,' Dad said.

'And it's not without risk. He's a bit of a difficult man. But he's probably the only one who can do it.'

'What's his name?' Dad said.

'Well, the man you want,' Frank said, 'is the Computer Wizard. But the less you have to do with him, the better. Get him round here, get him to put things right, and then get rid of him – if you can. Yes, I'm afraid that the Computer Wizard is the only one who can help you now. I'll give you his number, here.' He wrote FREE-PHONE WIZ on a notepad. 'And the best of luck. I'll find my own way out.'

With that Frank took off down the stairs and flew out of the front door as fast as he could go.

'Phew,' he said. 'I hope I don't get one of them every day.' He walked along the path towards his van when he remembered that there was something he hadn't told Michael's dad. He picked up a handful of gravel and threw it up at the spare bed – that is, at the study window. Dad opened the window and peered out.

'Yes!' he said.

'One thing, Mr Riggs, about the Computer Wizard – something I forgot to mention –'

'What about him?'

'He's not human.'

'Not what? Not human? What is he, then? An alien?'

'No, but he escaped.'

'From what?'

'A computer.'

'What do you mean?'

'I mean he used to be in a computer game called *Wizzy Wiz*, but somehow or other, he got out.'

'What?'

'Just thought I'd better tell you,' Frank said. 'So be careful.'

He got into his van, started the engine and drove off as quickly as his wheels would go.

13

The Computer Wizard

Dad looked at little Michael, who appeared to be day-dreaming. He tapped on the computer screen with his knuckle.

'Michael? Are you all right?'

Michael nodded. He was all right and yet he wasn't all right. He was starting to feel that he didn't actually want to come out of the computer now. In fact he might just wander off and see if he could find that Gumble.

'Michael,' Dad said. 'Don't go away. I think I might have the answer. The Computer Wizard. I'll ring him now.' He picked up the phone.

'Freephone Wiz, please,' Dad said to the operator.

'Putting you through now, sir,' she said. There

was a click then another voice spoke. It was an odd voice, a mechanical, artificial voice. The sort of voice you'd hear if a computer spoke to you.

'Hello,' the voice said. 'The Computer Wizard. What have you mucked up? Broken your computer, have you? Wrecked your disk drives? Caught a computer virus? Lost all your files? There's idiots everywhere, believe me. You could well be one of them.'

'Oh, good morning,' Dad said.

'Is it, now?' the Computer Wizard said. 'I wouldn't know. I've always got my nose in a computer myself. With the right computer, you could rule the world. But of course, you'd have to remember to plug it in first.'

'Well, it is about my computer, as a matter of fact. I've got a small problem with it.'

'Yes, that's what they all say. They all say it's a small problem, when what they mean is it's a whacking great big one.'

'I believe you know all about computers?'

'I should say so. I know them inside and out, you could say, yes, inside and out.' The Computer Wizard gave a mechanical cackle.

'My son's got stuck in the computer somehow, you see –'

'Wouldn't surprise me. Boys are like that. Get stuck in anything, boys will. Nothing but trouble.'

'Can you get him out?'

'I'll give it a try, but it'll cost you –'

'How much?'

'I'll tell you when I get there. What's your address?'

Dad told him.

'I'll be round,' the Computer Wizard said. 'Soon as I can. And don't turn the computer off, or you'll lose him. He's been messing round with the SPELLS program, I should think. In fact, it might be a good idea to make a copy of him, just to be on the safe side.'

'Make a copy of him?'

'Yes, copy him on to your floppy disk. You know how to do that, don't you?'

'Yes,' Dad said, 'I suppose so.'

'Do it then,' the Wizard said, and he hung up.

Dad put the phone down and stared at Michael. He reached for a floppy disk and put it into the disk drive.

'I'm just going to make a copy of you, Michael,' he said. 'It shouldn't hurt – I don't think. It's just a bit like recording a programme off the television on to the video, that sort of thing. It won't take a moment.'

Michael wasn't sure about this. He didn't know how he felt about there being a copy of him. How would people know who the real one was? What if, by some chance, the copy got out of the computer before he did? And went round wearing his clothes and eating his breakfast and sitting in his place at school? Or what if they both got out? Then there'd be two of them, two Michaels. They'd have to share a room. Yes, he'd have to share a room with himself and have a bath with himself. He'd have twice as many teeth to brush and two pairs of jeans to put on every morning instead of one and four legs instead of two. And he'd have to share his bed with himself – and that wouldn't be very comfortable, not two of him in the one bed.

But then, on the other hand, he'd always have someone to talk to and play with. He was hardly likely to fall out with himself, or fight with himself, or refuse to talk to himself. So it might not be so bad having a copy of himself after all.

The floppy disk whirred in the disk drive.

'Done it,' Dad said. 'Now that was quite painless, wasn't it?'

And it had been, too. Yet it felt funny, knowing that there was another one of you, copied on to a computer disk, another Michael there for emergencies. It was odd to have a spare. Still, Michael thought, it means that if anything terrible happens to me, I'll be all right. The thought comforted him as he waited for the Wizard.

The Computer Wizard wasn't long in coming. The first thing Dad heard was the sound of a motor bike tearing up the road and stopping outside the house. He looked out of the window and saw a figure getting off the bike and removing a crash helmet. A small man stood there, wearing a black leather jacket with a star on the back. He had a tufty beard and his long grey hair was tied in a pony tail. He had what looked like a wand sticking out of his top pocket. It was difficult to tell quite how old he was. In fact he was sort of timeless, like a clock that has stopped.

The Wizard looked up and saw Dad peering at him from the window.

'It's me. Computer Wizard,' he called. 'Is this the place with the boy stuck in the computer?'

Dad opened the window and shouted down.

'Yes, just come up. The door's not locked. We're up here in the study.'

The Computer Wizard looked doubtful.

'Are you sure that's a study?' he said. 'Looks more like a spare bedroom to me.'

'Of course it's not a bedroom,' Dad said indignantly. 'If it was a bedroom, it would have a bed in it. Well, it hasn't got a bed, it's got a desk. Therefore it's a study.'

The Wizard looked up at him. 'Not necessarily,' he said. 'Just because you put a desk into a bedroom, that doesn't turn it into a study, you know. I mean, suppose I went and put a desk in the swimming pool. That wouldn't turn the swimming pool into a study, would it? So why should it turn a bedroom into one? Answer me that.'

'Look,' said Dad. 'Are you going to stand down there all day arguing, or are you going to come up here and get my son out of this computer?'

'Two shakes,' the Wizard said. 'And before you can say "I'll be up there", I'll be up there.' Before Dad could work out what he meant, the Wizard was in the house, up the stairs and standing right beside him, peering at the computer.

Now that Dad could see him properly, the Computer Wizard looked very odd indeed. He wasn't smooth and round like most people, he was sort of lumpy and bitty, as if he was made out of lots of little dots. In fact he looked like a greatly enlarged computer figure. He looked at Michael in the computer screen.

'There's a boy in that computer,' the Computer Wizard said.

Michael waved and gave a faint smile.

'I know there's a boy in the computer,' Dad said. 'You don't need to tell me. I know that already, don't I? I'm not completely stupid.'

The Wizard flashed him a look.

'You're not completely stupid?' he said.

'No,' Dad said, testily. 'I am not completely stupid.'

'I see,' the Wizard said. 'So how stupid are you? A big bit stupid or just a little but stupid? Or a medium bit stupid?'

'I am not stupid at all,' Dad said, his face growing red.

'Then how come you can't get him out of there, eh?'

'That's different,' Dad said. 'That's just lack of experience.'

'Precisely,' the Wizard said. He stared at Michael and gave a little cackle. 'Stuck in there, are you?' he said gleefully. 'Not so nice is it, being inside a computer all the time?'

Michael shook his head. No, it wasn't so nice, to be honest. Not as nice as having your own room and Mum and Dad and sister. Your own bike and house and friends at school.

'You don't need to tell me what it feels like,' the Computer Wizard said. 'I know all about it. I was in one myself. For years I was stuck inside a computer. Bored out of my brains, I was. Bored, bored, bored and bored again.' He turned to Dad, his eyes glittering.

'Here,' he said. 'You're probably old enough to remember.'

'Remember what?'

'Aladdin, genies in bottles and magic lamps. Remember them, do you?'

Why, even Michael knew about them. You didn't have to be as old as Dad to know about

Aladdin. He had seen him at the pantomime and read about him in books.

'Well, it's all changed now, all been modernized,' the Wizard said. 'Once it was genies in bottles, now its wizards in computers. And there I was, stuck in a computer game, with no chance of getting out. Stupid game called *Wizzy Wiz* it was. Dull, dull, dull! It was so dull, it was like doing your dull times tables. One times dull is dull, you know, two times dull is double dull, three times dull is even duller. Nothing to talk to but the odd computer bug, or a dozy Gumble. Well, I didn't fancy that much, no thank you. Not hanging around with dozy Gumbles all day, having that lot follow you about the place. Got right on my nerves, that did.'

'So do you think you can get him out?' Dad said, feeling that the Wizard was wandering off the point again.

'No probs,' the Wizard said and he sat down at the desk. 'No problem at all. Absolutely probless. I can do anything with computers. I'm a computer wizard. *The* Computer Wizard in fact!'

'Do you know how he might have got in there?' Dad asked.

'Same way as I got out, I should think,' the Computer Wizard said. 'It's the SPELLS program.'

70

'SPELLS program?' Dad said.

Michael on the computer screen sat up and listened.

'Oh yes,' the Wizard said. 'There I was, stuck inside this smelly old computer, so I decided the only way to get out was to write my own SPELLS program. And that's what I did. It's full of special spells for getting in and out of computers. And so I got myself out and now I'm working on the Big One.'

'The Big One what?' Dad asked.

'The Big Extra Special SPELLS Program! When it's finished, they'd better watch out, that's all.'

'Who had better watch out?'

'Everyone and anyone,' the Wizard said. 'Anyone who upsets me, that'll be it. I'm going to type their names into the SPELLS program and press the button and whoosh!'

'Whoosh what?'

'They'll be deleted! Erased! Permanently got rid of.'

'What do you mean, deleted, exactly?'

'You know,' the Wizard said. 'Deleted. You know what happens when you delete something?'

'It isn't there any more.'

'That's right,' the Computer Wizard said. 'They won't be there any more. They'll be gone.'

'But – what will happen to them?' Dad said.

'What'll happen to them? You never see them again, that's what'll happen to them.' The Wizard cackled a terrible cackle and chortled so hard that he got the hiccups.

'I don't think that's very nice, actually,' Dad said.

'Then you'd better watch it then, hadn't you? Or I'll put your name on the list. And as soon as I get the Big SPELLS Program working – you'll be the first to go.'

Michael didn't like the sound of this. What right had this Wizard to go around deleting people and threatening them, just because they happened to tread on his foot, or tug his beard, or disagree with him?

And Dad wasn't too happy about it either.

14

In for a Spell

'Look,' Dad said, 'how come your SPELLS program is in my computer any way? What's it doing in there?'

'Oh, there's a few odd copies knocking about,' the Wizard said. 'Or you might find one on an old second-hand computer. Then what happens is that people try to use the computer dictionary. They type in SPELL and it sets the whole thing off. But don't worry, as soon as I get him out, I'll fix it for you so it won't happen again.'

'So is that all you have to do?' Dad said. 'It's that simple?'

'The cleverest things are always simple,' the Wizard told him. 'That's what's so clever about them. You only have to type SPELL INIT and whoever's sitting at the keyboard goes in. And then you type SPELL OUTOFIT to get them out. And if you want to get a particular person in, you just type their name first. Like, what's your name?'

Dad paused. He was reluctant to give the Wizard his real name in case he put him in the computer too.

'It's Sid,' he lied.

'Then if I wanted to put you inside the computer, all I'd have to type in would be SPELL SID INIT. And you'd be in there.'

'Well, I'd rather stay out here, if it's all the same to you.'

'Don't blame you,' the Wizard said. 'Didn't like it in there myself. As I said, dull, dull, dull.'

'So how did you get out?' Dad asked.

'Well,' the Wizard explained, pleased to have a chance to boast of his cleverness, 'I just flashed a message up on to the screen saying SPELL WIZ OUTOFIT. And this lady whose computer I was stuck in saw the message and thought it was something she had to do. So away she goes and types SPELL WIZ OUTOFIT and the next thing she knows, I'm out of the computer and sitting on her knee. It gave her quite a fright, I can tell you. It's the last thing people expect, you know, to suddenly have a wizard sitting on their knees.'

'I bet,' Dad said. 'What did she do?'

'What? Apart from scream you mean? Oh, well, I couldn't let her go round telling everyone that I'd escaped from her computer, they might have called the police.'

'So?'

'So I put her in it,' the Wizard said cheerfully.

'Put her in it?' Dad said.

'Yeah. I typed in SPELL MRS CONWAY INIT – that was her name, see, Mrs Conway – and in she went. Just like him.' He pointed at Michael.

'And she's still in there?' Dad said.

'I suppose so,' the Wizard said. 'As far as I know. It was a couple of months back now. We haven't really kept in touch.'

'A couple of months back? But – what about her husband, when he came home and found his wife wasn't there? And there was just this big wizard escaped from a computer, sitting in her place?'

'Well, he wasn't too pleased about it,' the Wizard admitted. 'So I put him in, too. SPELL MR CONWAY INIT. Very simple, see. It's all you have to do. A child could do it.' He pointed at Michael again and sniggered. 'In fact a child did do it, see?'

'But – but –' Dad was too flabbergasted to speak.

'And I put the cat in as well.'

'Mr and Mrs Conway and the cat?'

Now, Dad seemed to remember seeing something on the news about the Conways. About how they had mysteriously disappeared and had never been seen again.

'Yeah, I thought the cat would be company for them,' the Wizard said. 'I got fed up with him miaowing all over the place, so I put him in too. All you have to do is type SPELL CAT INIT and in he goes. Marvellous way of getting rid of cats it is. I'd recommend it to anyone. And then I got a few tins of cat food from the kitchen and typed in SPELL CAT FOOD INIT so he wouldn't be hungry. Only I forgot to do the tin opener. But there you are. You can't remember everything.'

'And so where are they now?' Dad asked.

'Still there, I suppose,' the Wizard cackled. 'Still inside the computer, wherever that may be. I took it down to Clarke's Cheap And Cheerful Computer Shop and sold it to him. I bought this leather jacket with the money and paid to get my wand painted. Smart, eh? Or what?'

Dad wondered if he should phone for the police. But he was afraid that if he did, the Wizard would just type SPELL COPPERS INIT and the police would end up in the computer too. Or maybe he'd type SPELL DAD INIT and Dad would be in there with them. In fact, what was to stop this awful wizard from typing SPELL WHOLE WORLD INIT and the whole world would end up inside the computer? He looked mad enough to do it. Dad decided he had to be stopped.

Michael, meantime, had been jumping up and down on the screen. They seemed to have forgotten all about him and he felt he had been stuck in there long enough. He wanted to get out. The Wizard noticed his impatience.

'I think he's getting a bit fed up in there,' he said. 'I'll get him out, shall I?'

'Please,' Dad said. 'I'd be most grateful.'

'It's five hundred quid,' the Wizard said.

'It's what?'

'Five hundred quid.'

'Five hundred quid,' Dad said. 'That's a bit steep.'

'I've got steep expenses,' the Wizard said. 'And if your own son isn't worth five hundred quid to you –'

'All right,' Dad said hastily. 'I'll get my cheque book.'

The Wizard rolled up his sleeves, flexed his fingers and went to type on the keyboard. He stopped, hesitated, his fingers poised over the keys.

'What's his name?' he asked.

'Michael,' Dad said.

The Wizard typed SPELL MICHAEL OUT-OFIT. And he pressed the RETURN key.

15

Back Out

There he was. Out. Full-sized and back to normal. And feeling most terribly hungry, but otherwise unscathed.

'I expect you feel hungry,' the Computer Wizard said. 'I did when I came out. I was so hungry I ate three tins of cat food and six tins of pilchards on toast.'

'Michael!' Dad helped him to his feet because he had landed on his bottom on the carpet – and gave him such a fierce hug, Michael thought that his ribs were going to crack.

'Hello, Dad,' he said. He hugged him back. 'I thought I was in there for ever.'

'Me too. Don't you ever do it again.'

'Thanks would only be polite,' the Wizard said.

'Oh yes, of course, thank you. Thank you very much.'

'And my cheque for five hundred quid would be even politer.'

'I'll get my cheque book,' Dad said.

'That's the second time you've said that,' the Wizard pointed out. 'But you haven't done it yet. And all talk and no cheque books makes Wiz a very angry boy, you know.'

'I'll do it now,' Dad said.

'Thank you very much again,' Michael said, feeling that it was best to be as polite as possible to the Wizard. Dad took his cheque book from a drawer of the desk.

'Not at all,' the Wizard said. 'It's worth it to me to find out where all the spare SPELLS programs are. I'm going to erase all the copies, so I'll have the only one. I'll just get rid of this one, get my cheque and I'll be off.'

Dad and Michael looked at each other. They both knew that something had to be done about this Wizard. He was a dangerous man and a menace to society and shouldn't be out on the loose. But how to stop him?

Michael had an idea.

'What did you say you were going to do?' he asked.

'Get this SPELLS program off your computer,' the Wizard said. Like all experts he loved telling people about what he was going to do next.

'Can I do it?'

'Oh, no, Michael,' Dad said. 'Not again. Don't you think you ought to leave well alone?'

'Oh, let him do it,' the Wizard said. 'You don't learn if you don't make mistakes.' He made room for Michael to sit down at the keyboard. 'I'll tell you what to type.'

'Ready,' Michael said.

'Right. Type DELETE ALL SPELLS,' the Wizard said, 'and then press RETURN.'

But Michael didn't type in DELETE ALL SPELLS. He typed in something else entirely. He rapidly typed SPELL WIZARD INIT and then he pressed the RETURN key before the Wizard could see what he had done. There was a flash and a groan, an explosion of green smoke, and the Wizard simply wasn't there any more.

'Where's he gone?' Dad said, looking about the spare bedroom – the study, that is – as the smoke began to clear. 'That Wizard, he was right here –'

'There he is, Dad,' Michael said, and pointed triumphantly at the computer screen. Now a tiny little Wizard, no bigger than a baked bean, was inside. He was hopping up and down and he looked angry enough to burst. Though you couldn't hear what he was saying, it wasn't hard to guess.

'Get me out of here!' the small figure in the computer yelled. 'Or I'll turn you into a squashed worm. I'll turn you into a blister. I'll turn you into a rubbish dump!'

'He seems a bit angry,' Dad said.

'Yes,' Michael agreed. 'It wouldn't do for him ever to get out again.'

'Then we'd better get rid of the Spells Program, I suppose.'

'Right,' Michael said and he began to type.

The little Wizard hopped up and down, so angry now that he had turned red all over. Even his grey beard was scarlet. 'Don't do that,' he yelled. 'I'll be stuck in here for ever.'

DELETE SPELLS PROGRAM Michael typed, and he pressed the RETURN key.

'Ahhh!' the little Wizard yelled. 'You're rotten, rotten, rotten. All of you, rotten. You're the rottenest lot I've ever known. You're so rotten you smell! You're rottener than all the rotten times table. Once rotten is rotten and twice rotten is rottener and you're even rottener than that. In fact you're so rotten . . .' and he ran off into the computer in a fury.

'That's it,' Michael said. 'We're safe. I don't half feel hungry Dad, you know.'

'Let's go downstairs,' Dad said. 'I'll make you some breakfast.'

They went down to the kitchen.

16

Babacadacra

When Mum returned home with Emily later that day, they were both delighted to find Michael out of the computer.

Emily's pleasure at finding her brother back to normal was slightly tinged with disappointment. She was now unable to charge her friends twenty pence each to come and see him.

'You could have stayed in another few hours,' she grumbled. 'Until everyone had been to look at you. But that's the trouble with brothers – they're so selfish. Could you go back in for a while?'

'No!' Michael snapped. 'I could not. If you're that keen on the idea, go and get stuck inside it yourself and I'll come and feed you bananas.'

Michael's mother was concerned to see that

he had on his trainers. She hadn't noticed them before.

She looked at him sternly.

'Michael,' she asked. 'Were you wearing your trainers inside the computer?'

'Pardon?' he said, munching hungrily on his fifth sandwich of the day.

'You aren't even supposed to wear your trainers in the house, Michael,' his mother continued. 'Let alone inside the computer! I suppose I'll have to go in there and vacuum up the mud now.'

'I wouldn't advise it,' Dad said. 'Anyway, you can't. Nobody will be getting stuck inside any computers ever again. We've fixed it, haven't we, Michael?'

And he gave him a wink.

'Yes, Dad,' Michael said, and he winked back.

Mum eyed them suspiciously.

'Exactly how?' she asked. 'Did you get Michael out?'

'Oh, you know,' Dad said airily. 'I just sort of – waved my magic wand.'

'Well, you must promise never to do such a thing again, Michael,' Mum said – as though he had been planning on making a habit of it. 'Once is quite enough for anyone. You must stay out of computers entirely from now on. If you really want to get stuck into something, go and get stuck into a good book.'

Michael and his father decided they wouldn't mention the whereabouts of the Computer Wizard to anyone else. It seemed best to keep it quiet somehow. It would be their secret. People didn't understand things like that. They either didn't believe you at all or thought you'd gone off your head.

Mum did wonder after a few days about the Wizard's crash helmet. She also asked Dad whose motor bike it was parked in their garden. Dad said he was looking after it for a friend. Then he drove it into town and gave it to the Oxfam shop and it was sold for charity.

Mr and Mrs Conway and their cat preyed on Michael's mind. He kept thinking about them, stuck inside their computer for ever, put in there by the Computer Wizard and unable to get out.

'Dad,' Michael said. 'Don't you think we ought to try and rescue the Conways?'

'Yes,' Dad said. 'I suppose we should. Only how? We don't even know where their computer is.'

'You don't think it might still be at Clarke's Cheap And Cheerful Computer Shop?'

'It's worth a try.'

They hurried over to Clarke's Cheap And Cheerful Computers. Mr Clarke greeted them cheerfully. Being cheerful cost him nothing.

'Mr Riggs,' he said. 'What can I do for you? Still got that boy in your computer, have you?

Worse than old ladies in lavatories are boys in computers. They'll be there from Monday till Saturday if you don't watch them.'

'No, he's out,' Dad said. 'This is him here.'

'How d'you do?' Mr Clarke nodded. He'd never actually met a boy who'd been stuck in a computer. 'I met someone who'd been on the telly once,' he said. 'But it's hardly the same.'

'Now,' Dad said. 'The thing is, we're looking for something. You wouldn't have a second-hand computer here? Brought in a few months ago? By a funny looking wizard type? A dotty looking sort of bloke?'

'Dotty looking? Now let me think,' Mr Clarke mused. 'Oh yes, I remember. Yes. I've still got it. Why, are you interested?'

'We might be,' Michael said. 'Can we try it out?'

Mr Clarke found the Conways' old computer at the back of the store. He plugged it in and turned it on.

'There you are,' he said. 'See what you think.' And he went to serve another customer.

'Go on, Michael,' Dad said. 'You do it.'

So he did. He sat at the keyboard and typed SPELL MRS CONWAY, MR CONWAY, CAT AND CAT FOOD OUTOFIT. Then he hit the RETURN key.

A moment later, a middle-aged man, a middle-aged woman, a rather elderly cat and several tins

85

of cat food – all looking remarkably unscathed by their ordeal – shot out of the computer and landed with a clatter on the floor.

The Conways looked around, rather bewildered.

'This isn't our house!' Mr Conway said. 'Where is this? And why do I feel so hungry?'

'Oi!' Mr Clarke said, turning to see them. 'Where did you lot come from? What's that cat doing here? Cats don't have computers. You can't bring moggies in here. Clear off.'

As Michael and his dad walked along the road with the Conways, they explained about the Computer Wizard, his plans to take over the world and how he was now safely locked up in their computer at home.

'I'm very relieved to hear it,' Mrs Conway said. 'I'm glad he's been locked up and you've thrown away the program. At least we'll never see him again.'

'Oh no,' Michael's dad said. 'Don't worry. We'll never see him again, will we, Michael? We've turned him off for good.'

But Michael wasn't quite so sure.

And he was right. Because the Wizard did come back.

For the next two weeks, every time they turned the computer on, there he was. A small angry figure, jumping up and down in a corner of the screen, waving his fist and wanting to be let out.

When they wouldn't let him out, he grew spiteful. He sneaked inside Dad's program for working out the gas bills and got the bug in there to mess up the calculations. When Dad went to print out how much money they owed, instead of getting a number all he got was 'SPLOD'.

He presumed this was some kind of rude word that wizards say to each other.

The next thing the Wizard did was to persuade all the Gumbles in the *Gumbles Go Next* computer game, to take their trousers off. When Dad turned the computer on again, instead of the usual grey screen, he was confronted by the Wizard and a long line of Gumbles, all showing him their bare bottoms.

'Disgusting!' he muttered. 'And extremely rude! Not to mention fat!'

And he turned them off.

Then the Computer Wizard vanished completely.

Or seemed to.

Except that Michael kept *thinking* he could see him. Out of the corners of his eyes. Just flitting around the edges of the computer screen.

And sometimes at night, he would see a light coming under the door, as if someone had turned the computer on. But whenever he went to investigate, the screen was dark and everything was quiet.

But one night, there was some typing on the screen.

ACRADABARA, it read.

And then,

BABACADACRA.

It was almost, Michael thought, as if someone was searching for a magic word – a magic password. But they couldn't quite remember how to SPELLIT.

Only the chances were, he guessed, that if you kept trying to spell a word, you would get it right eventually – even if only by accident.

Michael remembered the floppy disk then – the copy of him which his dad had made when he had still been inside the computer.

He went to check that it was still in the disk box. It was there. He carefully put a label on it and wrote on the label:

If I should disappear, it means the Wizard's got out again.

If you can't find me anywhere else, there's a copy of me in here.

Love, Michael.

And he went back to bed.

As he fell asleep, he thought he saw a large hairy Gumble and a man in a starry hat walking along the corridor, accompanied by a very odd-looking insect with sixteen feet – plainly some kind of bug. They tiptoed quietly past his bedroom door and headed for the stairs.

But Michael was really very tired by then. And was probably just imagining it.